To my wonderful Uncle Joe Pinkard
—A.J.

For Ellen Mager, Chelsea's "big sister"
—P.C.

A RICHARD JACKSON BOOK

Granddaddy says
when he was little
and the world was young

and only a few people had cars,
The Rolling Store would come
to the country at sunrise.

It would sit at the crossroads by the pine woods.
Then, the man who drove The Rolling Store
would sing:
      "We got it all.
      We got it all.
      The Rolling Store has got it all."

Granddaddy says the woods around The Rolling Store
would start singing out too.
Everybody from miles around would come.

Some on horses.
Most on foot.
It was always like a carnival then.

People laughing and talking,
buying what they needed and didn't need,
babies sitting in baskets
and kids jumping up and down
trying to be the first ones
in line at The Rolling Store
with all its wonders.

The sweet smells of pies and cakes,
the mystery of unseen things in barrels . . .
and the colors.
So many boxes and baskets of color.
These were miracle things, these baskets of color.

And when each person found what he wanted,
he'd keep close to The Rolling Store,
not ready to leave the magic.

It would always be:
    "See this."
    "Look at that,"
when people finished buying at The Rolling Store.
And the talk lasted all day long. . . .

But when the sun got low in the sky
and the shadows danced in the trees,
the man who drove The Rolling Store
would close the doors and sing:
     "We got it all.
     We got it all.
     The Rolling Store has got it all."

The people left would move slowly back home.
Some on horses.
Most on foot.

Then, Granddaddy says,
when the big store on wheels
had moved on into the dust
and everyone was gone,
but the world was still young . . .

if you listened close
you could almost hear
the trees still singing:

"We got it all.

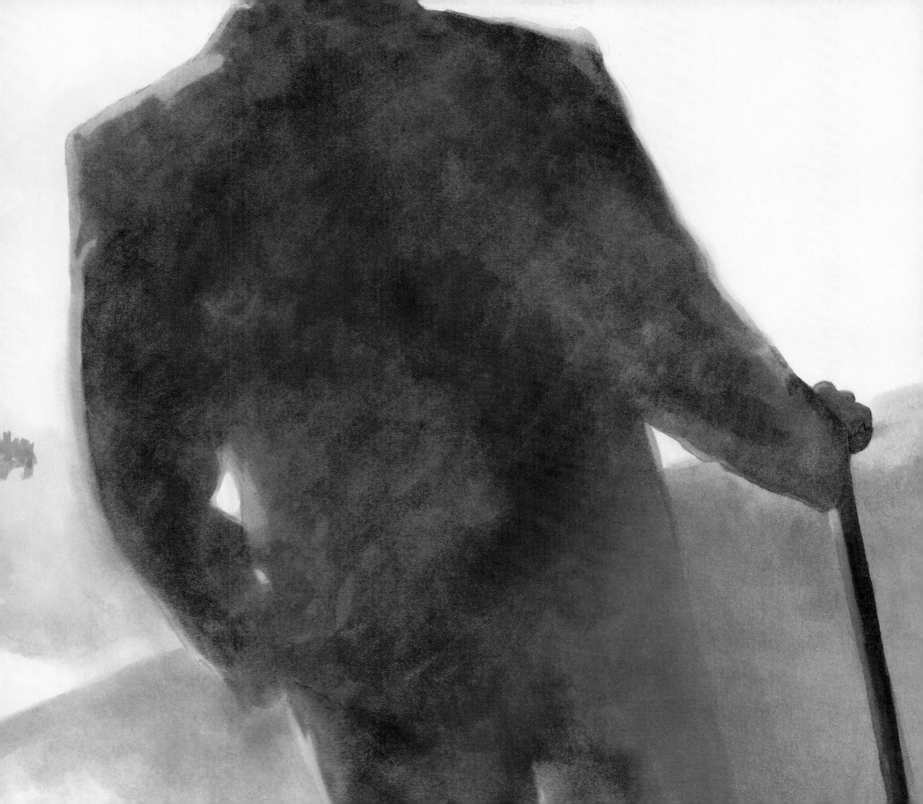

We got it all. . . ."

The song of

# The Rolling Store

story by **Angela Johnson**

paintings by **Peter Catalanotto**

Orchard Books  •  New York

*Thoughts to Leril and Takiah*
*and thanks to Maria Banks, Sue Allison,*
*and especially Jayne and Davianna—P.C.*

Orchard Books, 95 Madison Avenue, New York, NY 10016

Manufactured in the United States of America   Printed by Barton Press, Inc.
Bound by Horowitz/Rae   Book design by Jennifer Campbell

10 9 8 7 6 5 4 3 2 1

The text of this book is set in 16 pt. New Aster. The illustrations are watercolor and pencil reproduced in full color.

Library of Congress Cataloging-in-Publication Data
Johnson, Angela.   The Rolling Store / by Angela Johnson ; paintings by Peter Catalanotto.
    p.   cm.   "A Richard Jackson book"—Half t.p.
    Summary: As she and a friend are loading a wagon with cookies and fans they have made, a young girl repeats the
story of a wondrous Rolling Store that used to come to the country where Granddaddy lived when he was young.
    ISBN 0-531-30015-3. — ISBN 0-531-33015-X (lib. bdg.)    [1. Peddlers and peddling—Fiction.
2. Grandfathers—Fiction.]   I. Catalanotto, Peter, ill.   II. Title.   PZ7.J629Ro   1997   [E]—dc20   96-42151